DANNY ORLIS
AND THE
CONTRARY
MRS. FORESTER

DANNY ORLIS

AND THE

CONTRARY

MRS. FORESTER

BERNARD PALMER

Danny Orlis and the Contrary Mrs. Forester
© 2023 by Bernard Palmer
All rights reserved. First edition 1958.
Second edition 2024.

Cover image: Adobe Firefly
Character illustrations: John Ball
Editor: Charlene Miskimen

Aneko Press *Youth*

www.anekopress.com

Aneko Press, Life Sentence Publishing, and our logos are trademarks of Life Sentence Publishing, Inc.
203 E. Birch Street
P.O. Box 652
Abbotsford, WI 54405

JUVENILE FICTION / Religious / Christian / Action & Adventure
Paperback ISBN: 978-1-62245-978-0
eBook ISBN: 978-1-62245-979-7

10 9 8 7 6 5 4 3 2 1
Available where books are sold

CONTENTS

Ch. 1: In the Recreation Room................................1

Ch. 2: Bible School or U? 7

Ch. 3: Nothing to Be Alarmed About................................13

Ch. 4: Pressure................................21

Ch. 5: Party Plans 29

Ch. 6: A Mean Trick................................33

Ch. 7: An Angry Woman 37

Ch. 8: A Mom's Concern 45

Ch. 9: A Pastor's Interest 51

Ch. 10: An Unusual Visit 59

Ch. 11: A Dad's Concern................................63

Ch. 12: An Unexpected Blow 73

Ch. 13: All Hands Up! 81

Ch. 14: "A Terrible Mistake" 89

CHAPTER 1

IN THE RECREATION ROOM

It was a bitter February night in northern Minnesota. The blizzard had died out the day before, but the evidence of it was everywhere. Snow was piled high on either side of the walks and crunched protestingly under foot. Cars felt their way along the slippery streets, and across the way a determined home-owner struggled against the drift that imprisoned his garage door. The moon was out in all its frigid splendor to flood the little town of Cedarton with a pale, iridescent light.

Evergreens groaned in protest under their burdens of white, and sap freezing in the maples cracked in the still night air. The cold stung Danny Orlis' nostrils and bit at his cheeks as he left the library with a stack of books under his arm. He turned up his coat collar and hurried up the street.

Danny Orlis was a tall boy and sturdily built, like

the oak tree that stood guard on the library lawn. His face was ruddy from being outdoors in all kinds of weather, and his stride was strong and purposeful.

The cold went through Danny's coat, but he only walked faster until exertion warmed him. That was one of the things he had learned from his dad back on the Angle. In cold weather, keep moving. Not too fast, but not too slow either.

He didn't intend to stop at the Forester home as he approached the big brick house. He had a great deal of studying to do and an essay to start. But when he reached the house, he saw that there was a light in the basement. He paused momentarily. Kay hadn't been at the library. The chances were that she was in the Foresters' recreation room. On sudden impulse he went up to the door and knocked.

Mrs. Forester answered it. She looked ready for bed, and she was wearing a faded robe. When she saw Danny, she stiffened noticeably.

"I'm very sorry," she said coldly, "but Marilyn already has company this evening."

Before Danny could speak, Harold Forester came striding to the door and pushed past her. "Why, hello, Danny," he said pleasantly, "I'm glad to see you. There's quite a crowd in the basement, but I think you can find room. Go on down and make yourself at home."

Mr. Forester ushered Danny Orlis toward the basement.

"Really, Harold," Mrs. Forester snorted, "the basement is already crawling with people."

"That's why we fixed up the recreation room, Carrie," Harold answered. "The more kids we have here, the fewer there will be on the streets and in the hangouts up town."

Mrs. Forester dropped wearily into an overstuffed chair and dabbed at the corners of her eyes.

"I don't know what's gotten into you lately, Harold," she said, whining. "You used to share my dreams for Marilyn. She doesn't hang out with the children of any of my friends. She snubs them and ridicules the things they do. Yet you back her up."

"Marilyn would never snub anybody, Carrie," her husband protested. "You know that. It's just now she doesn't believe it's right to go to dances and movies and things of that sort. And she can't associate with those kids unless she does those things."

"If that isn't snubbing I'd like to know what you call it," Mrs. Forester bristled. "I used to think that I would be the happiest woman in the world when I could introduce my daughter to society and give her the advantages I never had when I was a girl. But she doesn't care a thing about that."

Mr. Forester went over and sat on the arm of her chair. "Marilyn doesn't want it that way, Carrie. And neither do I. I want her to live for the Lord Jesus."

"There you go, sticking up for her!" Tears flooded her eyes. "That's the way it's been since you – you got all mixed up in this ridiculous religious business. What I want or say doesn't matter anymore!"

Later in the evening, after the kids had left the Forester home, Mrs. Forester went down into the basement where Marilyn was putting away the last of the dishes. The older woman's eyes looked haggard and bloodshot, and her face was streaked where her makeup had run.

"I wish you'd entertain the guys and girls from our group of friends, Marilyn." Her voice was curt and frigid. "You're getting a reputation as a–a–. In our day we'd say you were getting a reputation as a wet blanket – a spoilsport."

"But Mom," Marilyn protested, "those other kids don't enjoy the things that I do. And I don't feel that it's right for me to do the things that they enjoy. It – it just wouldn't work for me to try to hang out with them."

"What your poor mother wants doesn't matter at all to you anymore, does it, Marilyn?" She moved closer to her daughter and was staring piteously at her.

"Of course it does, Mom," Marilyn answered. "I want you to be happy about the things I do and the kids I hang out with. I'll tell you what I'll do. I can't go their way, but I'll invite them down here for Bible Club sometime. Is that all right?"

Mrs. Forester straightened and brushed defiantly over her eyes with the back of her hand. "That isn't why I came down here. I came to see if you wanted to go to Minneapolis with me Saturday to start buying your school clothes. I sent yesterday for your application for entrance to the U."

"But Mom," Marilyn asked, "didn't – didn't Dad talk with you about college?"

The older woman stared at her blankly. "Talk to me about college?" she echoed. "It's always been agreed that you're to attend the university where your father and I went."

Marilyn swallowed hard. "I have been talking to Dad," she said hesitantly. "He's going to talk to you about it, but I guess he – he just hasn't gotten around to it. You see, I don't want to go to the university."

'You don't want to go to the U? Just where do you want to go to school?"

"Right here in Cedarton. I'd like to attend the new Cedarton Bible Institute."

Mrs. Forester's face went ashen. Her lower lip trembled momentarily. She tried to speak but for a moment she could not.

"Marilyn," she managed at last, "there'll be none of that foolishness. I have put up with all of this religious business I intend to. Marilyn Forester, you will go to the school I pick out. Do you understand?"

CHAPTER 2

BIBLE SCHOOL OR U?

Danny Orlis and his brother, Ron, walked to school together next morning.

"Kirk was telling me that you've definitely decided to go to Cedarton Bible Institute next fall," Ron said.

"That's right."

"I guess maybe you decided to do the right thing," the younger brother continued doubtfully, "but Tim is sure going to do some crowing. He's already telling the guys that you just don't have it when it comes to football. He even says that the only reason Crestwood offered you a scholarship was because they thought it would help them to land him."

Danny glanced away.

"He wouldn't do that, Ron. He's a friend of mine. A good friend."

"You just don't know him, that's all." Ron's eyes

flashed. "He's doing plenty of talking. And it makes me angry. You're a better football player than he is."

"Now, Ron," the older boy said, "it isn't very Christian of us to be talking about Tim this way."

They walked up the street together.

"Danny," Ron blurted, "I'm going to see that you're entered in that 'Most Popular Guy' contest out at school."

Danny turned.

"I'm not interested in that contest, Ron," he said. "It's a joke."

His brother's eyes flickered. "But I'm interested. And it's not a joke. I can tell you this much. I'm not going to have Tim Barton think that he's the only big shot in Cedarton."

Danny promptly forgot all about the contest, but Ron went directly to school and entered his brother in it.

That night Danny and Kay and the others who were planning to attend Cedarton Bible Institute gathered at the Forester home.

"I'm sure that our grades are all right," Danny said, "and that we'll get the recommendations we need. But we ought to get our applications in so they'll hold space for us. From what I hear that school is going to be so popular that we might not be able to get in if we wait."

Kay turned to Marilyn. "Are you going to apply at the same time the rest of us do?" she asked.

"I'm not sure," Marilyn Forester replied hesitantly. "Mom insists that I go to the university where she and Dad went."

"You'd better go to school here in Cedarton too," Danny told her.

Marilyn swallowed and blinked her eyes rapidly. "You'll all pray for me about school, won't you?"

When they all finished eating about 9:30 and went home, Marilyn went upstairs to talk with her mom.

"Have you thought any more about my going to school here in Cedarton?" she asked, walking into the kitchen where her mom was cleaning up.

Mrs. Forester's face went pale beneath the heavy coat of makeup.

"You – you aren't serious about going to that – that Bible Institute or whatever it is, are you?"

Marilyn pulled up a chair and sat down.

"I was never any more serious about anything in my life, Mom. All the kids I hang out with are going to school here, at least for two years."

"From what I hear," her mom said acidly, "you've been getting all the Bible training you need."

"But Mom, if I go into full-time service, I'll have to have Bible and Christian Education courses."

"I was hoping you'd go to the U and that my old sorority would pledge you, Marilyn." Her voice was trembling a little.

"But I don't want to join a sorority, Mom," Marilyn protested. "I want to go to a school where they will help me to make Christ mean even more in my life than He does now and where they will help me to learn how to do a better job of living for Him."

Mrs. Forester was silent while the clock in the hall struck 10 o'clock. "I've wanted so many things for you, my dear," she said, laying her hands across Marilyn's slim fingers. "I don't want to live your life for you, but I don't want to see you let all the best of life pass you by either. I want you to have fun. I want you to enjoy yourself."

Marilyn looked at her mom pleadingly. "Won't you think it over, Mom?" she asked at last. "I want to do what you and Dad want me to. But I would like to go to school here in Cedarton. I'd like that more than anything else."

Mrs. Forester looked up and blinked back her tears.

"I'll think it over for a day or two, Marilyn, if that's what you want."

It seemed to Marilyn that the rest of the week would never pass. She talked with her dad about going to school at Cedarton and he promised to talk to her mom about it.

"You know the Lord would want you go to a school like the Institute," he said. "If you keep on praying and trusting, it will work out all right."

But Marilyn was far from certain that everything would work out all right. Her mom spoke to her politely enough. In fact it seemed as though she went out of her way to be kind and considerate of Marilyn and her friends. But every time she mentioned the Bible Institute, Mrs. Forester's face clouded. Finally, Friday night came, and Marilyn went into the living room where her mom was sitting alone.

"Mom," she began hesitantly, "you said you would give me your answer about the school tonight."

"I've decided that it's up to you," her mom said in a small voice. "I want you to be happy. It doesn't matter about me or the plans I've been making down through the years. I don't count for anything anymore."

"Don't say that, Mom!"

"But you know what I want for you." Her voice was strained and far away. "If you really meant what you said just now, you'd go to the university without saying another word."

The young girl looked at her mom in bewilderment.

"Your father has been talking to me about this all week," Mrs. Forester said at last. "I told him this morning that I wasn't going to say anything more. If you're determined to ruin your life by going to that Bible Institute, there isn't anything more I can say." Her voice broke.

Marilyn stared at her helplessly.

A strange, blank expression came into Mrs. Forester's eyes. She got slowly to her feet and started to walk across the floor. Then without warning, she staggered two or three steps, gave a weak little moan and, leaning heavily on the couch, she began to sink slowly.

"Mom!" Marilyn cried, running toward her. But before the frightened girl could reach her, Mrs. Forester had fallen to the floor.

CHAPTER 3

NOTHING TO BE ALARMED ABOUT

Marilyn Forester ran quickly to her mom's side and shook her.

"Mom!" she cried.

Mrs. Forester lay motionless. Her eyes were closed, but the lids flickered slightly. Marilyn shook her again. Then, clumsily, she got to her feet and called her dad. Her dad wasn't answering! Her breath was coming in short, quick gasps as she dialed their family doctor.

"Don't try to move her, Marilyn," the physician ordered. "I'll be right over." With that he hung up and she was alone again.

From somewhere she remembered that a person who was unconscious should be kept very warm. Quickly she went into the bedroom and came out with a heavy comforter. As she did so she saw her mom's eyelids move again, ever so slightly.

"Mom!" she exclaimed again. "Mom! Speak to me!"

Marilyn shook her frantically, but the older woman still lay with her eyes tightly closed and her arms limp and lifeless. The frightened girl's heart sank within her.

By this time Dr. Benton came in briskly. Without taking off his coat he knelt beside Mrs. Forester and examined her.

"Has she been like this very long, Marilyn?" he asked when he had finished.

"It happened just a minute or two before I talked with you."

Dr. Benton took Mrs. Forester's pulse and then listened for a long while to her heart with his stethoscope.

"What is wrong?" Marilyn asked.

Without answering, the doctor continued his examination. In a moment or two Mrs. Forester opened her eyes. They flickered faintly and a weak little groan escaped her lips.

"I'm all right," she protested, moving slowly as though to sit up. She smiled faintly as her daughter put out her hand in protest.

The family doctor poured a few small white pills into a bottle and wrote instructions for taking them on the label.

"You'd better stay in bed until I get to see you and finish my examination tomorrow, Mrs. Forester."

* * * *

Ron Orlis began to campaign for Danny. He talked with all the guys at school and had Roxie talking to the girls.

"I think we've got a good chance of getting Danny elected," he said to his twin sister. "A lot of the guys are fed up with the way Tim is bragging all the time."

"But he's awfully cute."

"Cute?" Ron snorted. "Is that all you girls can think of? It doesn't make any difference what kind of a jerk a guy is. Just so he's cute!"

In the corridor that afternoon Tim Barton stopped Danny.

"I understand that you've entered the 'Most Popular Guy' contest," Tim said, trying to mask his disdain.

"Ron entered me," Danny answered. "He told me that he was going to, but I didn't think he'd do it."

"It doesn't make much difference. Whether I win or not doesn't matter to me, but so many of the kids are working for me that I don't think you've got a chance." Tim turned. "They seem to think that Crestwood contract of mine makes me a big shot."

The tone in his voice made Danny Orlis cringe.

* * * *

Marilyn followed the doctor into the living room.

"I don't think there's anything to be alarmed about, Marilyn," Dr. Benton said, smiling. "Her heart is good, and her blood pressure is normal. I don't think you need to worry about it."

The next morning Mrs. Forester protested that she felt all right, but her face was white and drawn. Marilyn brought breakfast to her on a tray and sat on a chair beside the bed while she ate.

"I've decided that I'm going to the university, Mom," she said after a time. "I feel that I owe it to you – to you and Dad."

"But Marilyn," her mom protested, "I won't let you do that. You want to go to the Bible Institute, and I can't stand in your way."

"But Mom," Marilyn countered, "I've decided that I'd better go to the U."

Mrs. Forester shook her head firmly. "I got to choose my school," she said. "I want you to choose yours."

* * * *

Mrs. Forester met Danny at the door.

"Why, you're Danny Orlis, aren't you? I've heard Marilyn talk so much about you. I didn't really associate you with the name until she told me that you were coming over this evening. We're so glad to have you."

Marilyn came into the living room just then, and she and Danny went down to the recreation room.

"Have you talked with Tim about that silly contest?" Danny asked.

Marilyn shook her head. "To tell you the truth, we haven't been going out together very much lately. It's been at least a month since I've even had a date with him."

They were still talking about Tim when Mrs. Forester came down the stairs with a tray of cookies and hot chocolate.

"I thought perhaps you guys would be hungry," she said, smiling at Danny.

"You didn't need to do this, Mom. I could have fixed a sandwich or something after a while."

"I wanted to do it. I want your friends to feel that they are welcome here."

They finished eating and played ping pong, and finally ended the evening sitting on the floor in front of the fireplace playing Scrabble with Mrs. Forester looking on and giving advice. When the time came for Danny to go home, he got up reluctantly.

"I certainly want to thank you," he said to Mrs. Forester and Marilyn. "It's been great."

"Come over any time," Marilyn's mom told him. "We'll be delighted to have you."

Marilyn smiled and held out her hand. "That goes for me too, Danny."

Danny Orlis walked home slowly. It was a funny thing, but he had never thought much about Marilyn before. She was certainly a lot of fun!

He hadn't realized how much he had been neglecting the Bible Club and youth group while he was trying to decide which college to attend until now that his decision had been made. He was surprised when Marilyn called him the next day and asked him to talk to Karen Meyer about going to youth group.

"We've got to get some of those sophomores into our group," she explained.

Danny went down into the living room and tried to talk to Karen, but she didn't act interested. She gave no indication that she was going, but when he got ready she slipped into her coat and walked with him to the door.

"I'll walk over with you."

"That's fine," Danny told her. "You're picking a good time to start too. We're going to have a party in a couple of weeks."

"I know," Karen told him shyly.

She sat on the back row during the meeting and didn't take part in the discussion, but as soon as the program was over she called Kay aside.

"I – I'd like to talk to you a minute," the younger girl said softly, with a quick look toward the rest of the group.

"Let's go in here," the missionary girl said, guiding her fifteen-year-old companion into the kitchen where they were alone. "Now," she went on, "what was it you wanted to talk to me about?"

"It's the party," Karen continued hesitantly.

"We certainly want you to come," Kay said.

"That isn't it," the younger girl answered. "It's just that Tom Bailey asked me to go with him. I don't know whether I should or not."

"What do your parents say about your dating?" Kay asked.

"Mom always said she wanted me to wait until I was sixteen," Karen answered, "but I'll be sixteen next month."

"Tom is a fine Christian boy."

Kay Milburn smiled warmly. "Everyone's waiting for me, Karen. But I'll stop over by your place tomorrow evening after school and we'll talk about it. Okay?"

"You won't say anything to Danny or any of the others about it, will you, Kay?"

It had taken Kay a little longer with Karen than she thought it would and the other kids had all gone out into the hall. Quickly she turned out the lights and pushed through the swinging door just in time to see Danny and Marilyn go out the front door together.

"Danny," she started to call out, then checked herself suddenly.

Marilyn and Danny were laughing at something one of them had said. They didn't even miss her!

For a long while Kay stood at the foot of the stairs, staring hard at the floor. Then she got into her coat and went out alone.

CHAPTER 4

PRESSURE

Danny Orlis and Marilyn hurried out into the bitter night air and walked briskly up the street.

"I was so glad that you were able to get Karen to come to youth group tonight," Marilyn said. "That's the first time she's been with us."

"I wasn't sure whether she was going to come or not."

They walked on for several minutes.

"The one who has surprised me lately is my mom," Marilyn told him. "It's so wonderful to have her like she is."

Mrs. Forester met them at the door. "Good evening, young man," she said, smiling. "You're getting to be a regular fixture around here, aren't you?"

The Orlis boy grinned self-consciously and removed his hat and coat.

"Some of the other kids will be coming over before long," Marilyn said, leading Danny into the living room. "Why don't we sit here by the fireplace until they start coming?"

"What would you like this evening, Marilyn?" Mrs. Forester called in to them. "Hot chocolate or malts?"

Marilyn looked at Danny. "What would you like?"

"Either one sounds fine to me."

In a few minutes the rest of their friends began to come, and Marilyn and Danny went down to the basement and got out some games.

"Is everybody here?" Marilyn asked, glancing around.

"Everybody but Tim and Kay. Were they coming?"

Marilyn turned to Danny. "Kay was coming over here tonight, wasn't she?"

"I didn't expect Tim, but I certainly thought Kay would come. She was at youth group."

"I'm going to phone her," Marilyn said. "Maybe she didn't understand that she was to come over here with us."

In a few minutes Marilyn Forester was back. Danny went over to her. "Is Kay coming?"

She shook her head. "She told me she didn't feel like coming tonight. But, Danny, she sounded to me as though she had been crying."

The young woodsman turned back to the game, but he had lost interest. Poor Kay! Perhaps she had gotten bad news from home.

Mrs. Forester made tall, frosty chocolate malts and served them later in the evening. And shortly afterward the kids got into their coats and began to file out the door.

When they had all gone, Marilyn turned to her mom.

"Thank you very much for making snacks for us tonight," she said appreciatively. "You didn't have to do that, you know. We could have fixed something."

"I'm glad you liked it, Marilyn. I'm going to do everything I can to make your friends happy here."

The girl threw her arms about her mom and kissed her impulsively. Mrs. Forester sniffled a little.

"I want to do all I can to be nice to your friends," she went on slowly. "But I can't help wishing that you would spend at least some of your time with the young people whose mothers are in my set of friends."

"I'd like to, Mom," Marilyn told her gently. "For your sake. But we just don't do the same things. All most of them want to do is go to a dance or park on some lonely road."

Mrs. Forester took a tissue from her pocket and dabbed at her eyes. "You must be misjudging those kids, Marilyn. They're good, decent guys and girls. You've got the wrong impression because you think some of the things they do are wrong. I wish you weren't so snobbish."

"I don't want to be snobbish, Mom," Marilyn said, laying her hand on her mom's arm.

"Your father and I fixed the recreation room for you. I would think that the least you can do is to entertain the young people whose moms are in my club."

Marilyn sat for a time staring into the fireplace. "I'd like to have those kids over, Mom," she said, "if they would enjoy the same things that I do."

"Why don't you try?" Mrs. Forester asked, seizing on the thought. "You could invite them over some evening when there's nothing going on at school and just have the kind of a good time that you have with your own group. I know you'd find that they'd enjoy it as much as your other friends do."

* * * *

The next morning Kay went to school at the usual time. She was somewhat surprised to find Danny standing at her locker waiting for her.

"We missed you last night at Marilyn's," he said.

"I didn't feel like going."

"I thought maybe there was something wrong." She shook her head.

"Marilyn thought you might have gotten bad news from home or something."

* * * *

That evening after school Kay and Karen went down to the shop. They sat in a booth toward the back, had a dish of ice cream, and talked.

For a few moments Karen giggled nervously and joked about the party, saying she had decided not to go. But finally, Kay settled her down and got her to talk seriously.

"I – I've got to give Tom an answer tomorrow," she said at last. "And I don't know what to tell him."

"Would you like to go to the party with him, Karen?" Kay asked.

She nodded and her cheeks colored faintly.

"What does your mom think about it?"

"I don't know. I haven't said anything to her about it yet."

"That's the first thing you ought to do," Kay told her. "Talk to your mom and see if it's all right with her. This is something you want to be very careful to let your parents know about and be sure that they approve."

"I'd sort of thought," Karen went on, "that if I did decide to go, I'd tell Tommy I'd meet him outside the church or maybe at the library."

"Oh, don't do that!" Kay answered. "Don't get into the habit of meeting your dates uptown somewhere. The guys will think more of you, and your parents will trust you more if you have the guys come to the house and meet your mom and dad. You mustn't try to deceive them."

Karen had been worrying about how she would talk to her mom about the party, but she needn't have worried. When everybody was at the supper table her younger brother, Kirk, looked about and grinned.

"I know something about Karen," he said, laughing.

She lowered her gaze and became suddenly interested in the intricate design around the outside rim of her plate.

"I know something about Karen," Kirk sang out again. "About Karen and Tommy Bailey."

She looked up, her eyes blazing. "You hush up, Kirk Meyer! Don't you say another word!"

Mr. Meyer glanced at his foster daughter. "What's this all about, Karen?" he asked. "It sounds interesting."

Karen's cheeks were scarlet. "It – it –. That Kirk!" she cried.

"Who is this Bailey guy?" Mr. Meyer continued. "I think we'll have to look into this, don't you, Danny?"

"Oh, I don't have to look into it!" Danny said. "I know him already."

Roxie turned to face Karen. "Do you mean you're going to that party with a boy?" she asked seriously. "What fun will that be?"

"Yeah," Kirk laughed, keeping one eye on Karen and one eye on the nearest exit. "She's going there with Tom Bailey, all right. I heard her talking to Kay about it."

"There's nothing so wrong about that," Mr. Meyer said. "I guess there are a lot of girls who've gone with boys to church parties."

"Know what I'm going to do, Dad?" Kirk asked. "I'm going to tag along. I'll wait until Tommy comes here for her and I'll follow along right behind them. I'll go every place they go."

"Kirk Meyer!" Karen exploded indignantly. "If you do! If you dare!"

"Don't let them tease you, Karen," said Mrs. Meyer,

smiling gently. She turned to Danny. "Do you know this Tom Bailey?"

"Sure," Kirk broke in. "Everybody in town knows Tom Bailey. He's the orneriest kid in school."

"Kirk!" Mrs. Meyer retorted firmly. "That will be enough out of you." She turned back to Danny. "Do you know him? Is he a nice boy?"

"He's a nice Christian guy," Danny told her.

"Well, then, Karen," Mrs. Meyer said to her daughter, "I think it would be very nice if you went to the party with him. That is, if you want to."

"Oh, she wants to all right!" Kirk put in quickly. "She's just crazy to go to the party with him!"

"Kirk," Mr. Meyer said, sobering, "your mom told you to quit teasing Karen."

"But she is," he retorted. "I heard her say so."

"That's enough," Mr. Meyer ordered sharply. "If you can't learn to mind, you'll have to leave the table."

"And that goes for all the rest of you," Mrs. Meyer put in, looking straight at her husband. "Let's not hear any more teasing out of any of you."

Mr. Meyer grinned crookedly.

CHAPTER 5

PARTY PLANS

Talk of the contest mushroomed in the days that followed. Several years before, the contest started as a joke and had become an annual affair. The guys campaigned laughingly and the crowning was usually the most hilarious event of the year. It would probably have stayed that way had Ron not campaigned so vigorously. His activity infuriated Tim.

"I tell you, Danny," the Barton boy said nastily, "I think it's mighty sneaky of you to put your brother up to all that stuff."

"But I haven't put Ron up to anything, and I'm going to put a stop to this contest thing. It doesn't mean anything anyway."

"It isn't doing you any good to lie like that. You're not fooling me. You're jealous because I'm going to Crestwood and you're not. You think that you're going to show me up in this contest. Well, I'm going to teach you a lesson you won't soon forget."

Danny Orlis' hands clenched convulsively.

"Take it easy, Tim!" he said softly.

Tim Barton snorted and turned away.

At youth group that night, Tim was absent again. Kay asked Danny about him on the way home.

"I wish there were something we could do to get him interested in Bible Club and youth group again," she said. "He's such a new Christian. I'm afraid he'll drift from the way he ought to live if he doesn't stay under the influence of the church."

"Maybe we could get him to come over to Marilyn's some night. He does like to play ping pong," Danny suggested.

"Yes, it's worth a try. He used to go there. In that way he would still be with the same people and he might start coming to youth group again."

Tim was not interested in going to Marilyn's, but Danny and his friends continued to go at every opportunity. Her mom treated them with studied kindness, a strangely exaggerated kindness that somehow made Danny feel a little uneasy, as though it were only an act.

Nevertheless, the young woodsman enjoyed going over and playing ping pong or Scrabble with Marilyn or just sitting and talking with her. With her mom unsaved and determined that she wasn't going to the Bible school, she was having a rough time of it. Poor kid.

But whether Danny was the only one who went over to see Marilyn, or whether everyone flocked in, Mrs. Forester was exceedingly polite. She always brought down snacks about 9:30 or 10:00 p.m. and joked a little with the kids as they ate.

"I want you all to feel completely at home," she said for the fifth or sixth time as they were leaving. "It's so good to know that Marilyn is associating with such fine young people who have such – such high standards."

When they were gone that evening Mrs. Forester turned to Marilyn. "We talked about a party for the children of my friends," she said, "but we didn't do any more about it. What have you decided, dear?"

"I was just waiting for you to set a time that would be convenient. It sounds like fun."

"I know it would be," her mom said, sitting down before the fireplace and motioning her daughter down beside her. "I just know it would be, but there is one thing that I've been wondering about, Marilyn. If you did have them, you wouldn't embarrass them, would you?"

"What do you mean, Mom?"

"You wouldn't play all those religious songs," she went on, "and expect them to read the Bible and sing those choruses, or whatever you call them, and pray, would you?"

Marilyn shook her head. "No," she answered, "I'm sure they wouldn't enjoy those things."

Marilyn had wanted to invite Danny and some of the other kids from youth group at the same time, but her mom was against it.

"It wouldn't be best to mix the groups," she said. "Not that I have anything against your friends, mind you. But, after all, there's so much difference in their position and social standing and everything."

Mrs. Forester bought the invitations and she and Marilyn filled them out the next evening. They cleaned the basement and put up some decorations and bought ice cream from the neighborhood grocery.

"There," her mom said, as they finished baking the cakes and made the last of the sandwiches. "This is going to be the finest party you have ever given. And I know you're going to find that these young people will enjoy it just as much as your other friends would. They enjoy good times too, and you'll find them a lot of fun if you just give them a chance."

"I've really been looking forward to this party," Marilyn told her happily, "more than any I've had for a long while."

Mrs. Forester beamed.

CHAPTER 6

A MEAN TRICK

There was a committee meeting that evening at the place where Kay stayed, and when it was over Danny and Kay went down to the shop for a malt.

"Well," the Orlis boy said, as they walked into the store and found a booth, "I suppose Marilyn's party is getting under way about now. Wish we'd been invited, don't you?"

She looked up at him, her eyes clouded. "You've certainly become interested in Marilyn and her parties all of a sudden," she said. She had wanted it to be a joke, but somehow her words came out harsh and bitter.

Danny was surprised. He stood there a moment, turning red, then took off his coat and sat down in the booth opposite her. What was she driving at anyway?

They had only been in the shop a moment or two and were just giving their orders to the waitress, when the front door opened and a laughing, loud-talking bunch of guys and girls came pushing in.

"Look, Danny!" Kay said softly. "Aren't those the kids who were supposed to have been at Marilyn's party?"

Danny turned a little as the crowd came trooping back to the booths.

"I think it's a dirty trick," Dick Bivens was saying loudly. "How's she going to get any stars in her crown if she doesn't get us over there to preach to us?"

For an instant or two Kay stared at Danny. A hurt look came into her eyes.

"Oh, Danny!" she exclaimed. "Isn't that awful? They all called Marilyn and told her they would be coming. Now they're not going to show up!"

Danny and Kay could scarcely believe what they had overheard.

"They must be joking," Kay whispered softly. "They wouldn't let Marilyn and her mom think they were coming and go to all that work preparing everything and then not show up."

"What do you suppose Marilyn's doing now?" the blond girl with Dick asked.

Dick laughed boisterously. "She's probably sitting down in the basement with a Bible in one hand and a hymnbook in the other wondering what happened to the poor lost sinners she was going to preach to."

"I'd like to be a little mouse in the corner," the blonde snickered. "I'd give anything to see the look on her face when she finally realizes we're not showing up."

"I just thought of something," Dick said eagerly. "Why don't we phone Marilyn? We'll tell her we're from the *Minneapolis Tribune* and would like a report on her party for the paper."

"I dare you," the blonde challenged. "I double dare you!"

"We'll tell her we've got a photographer along," Dick continued, laughing so hard he could scarcely talk, "and that we want to come out and take some pictures!"

"You're afraid to," Don Bridges retorted. "You wouldn't dare!"

"Just wait until I finish this malt," Dick told them, "and we'll see whether I dare or not."

"I've never heard anything so cruel," Kay whispered, leaning forward and speaking softly to Danny.

"Neither have I. It makes a guy feel like going over and telling them off!"

"That wouldn't do any good."

"You just wait until I get through with this malt," Dick repeated, boasting. "I'll show you whether I'm afraid to phone over there or not."

"What should we do, Danny?"

"I think we ought to go and tell Marilyn and her mom what's happening," he said, "before this crazy bunch calls and makes things worse."

Kay got to her feet and Danny helped her into her coat. "It's going to be awfully hard."

As they started past the booths one of the guys called to Danny. "Come over here, Orlis," he said.

Danny turned and saw that it was Dick. "I want to talk to you for a minute."

"Sure thing." He stopped and turned to face them.

"There's just one thing I want to know," Dick said, grinning. The other kids in the booth snickered. "How come you didn't go to Marilyn's party? Is she so religious that even you don't dare to go over there?"

"If I'd been invited to the party I'd have gone," Danny said coldly. "I'm not in the habit of accepting invitations and not showing up," and with that Danny turned on his heel and left.

CHAPTER 7

AN ANGRY WOMAN

Kay Milburn stood in the doorway at the Forester home and hesitantly told Marilyn and her mom that the kids they had invited to the party weren't coming.

"I thought I'd better come over and tell you what Danny and I overheard in the shop so you wouldn't keep on looking for them or wonder what happened."

"No!" Mrs. Forester protested, half rising in her chair. "It can't be true! You've made this up as a mean, nasty joke. You don't mean it!"

"But it is true, Mrs. Forester," Kay said miserably. "They all got together and decided not to come. Danny and I both heard them."

"You're joking," Marilyn's mom insisted numbly. The color had left her cheeks and her fingers tightly gripped the arms of the chair. "They wouldn't do this to me."

"It is true, all right," Marilyn put in. Her lips were trembling uncertainly and her face was ashen. "I overheard some of the kids talking in school today. At the time I didn't think anything about it. Now I know they were talking about the party tonight."

There was a long, breathless silence. Kay stared first at Marilyn and then at Mrs. Forester, who suddenly looked gaunt and very tired. Finally the older woman turned in sudden anger and pounced on Kay.

"If those young people decided not to come to the party tonight," she snapped, "it's because somebody gave them the wrong idea of what the party was going to be like!"

Her gaze was riveted on the missionary girl's face. Kay cringed under the force of the accusation.

"I should have known that you and that Danny Orlis and your crowd wouldn't let Marilyn associate with her own social class without a struggle," the older woman lashed, her voice quavering. "I should have known you'd make them think our party was going to be so – so religious that they wouldn't enjoy themselves!"

"I – I don't know what you mean," Kay said, faltering. "We didn't have anything to do with it."

"You don't have to lie to me! Don't add that to your sins. You thought that if they came and enjoyed themselves it wouldn't be long until you wouldn't get to use our recreation room. I know your kind! You were jealous!"

"Oh, Mom!" Marilyn broke in miserably. "Don't make things any worse. Kay and Danny and the others didn't have a thing to do with this. Why, they didn't even know about the party until this afternoon. And besides, they wouldn't try to ruin it for us. They wouldn't want to hurt me. They're my friends."

Her mom started to speak again but stopped and swallowed hard. Her lips were quivering, and huge tears hung on her eyelashes above her flushed cheeks.

"I – I've tried my best to put up with you, Kay Milburn," she continued, her voice breaking. "I've tried to be nice to you and the other religious fanatics who keep coming over here. I spent – I don't know how much – for ice cream and sandwiches and cold drinks, just to make you and your sponging friends happy."

The two girls looked at one another helplessly.

"And this is the thanks I get," Mrs. Forester said. "You've talked to the boys and girls she should rightfully be hanging out with. You've convinced them that this party would be too religious for them. You deliberately frightened them into not coming."

Kay's face was crimson to the roots of her soft blond hair.

"I – I hope you don't believe that, Mrs. Forester," she said earnestly. "Honestly, we didn't say a word to any of them. In fact, we didn't know about the party until this afternoon and didn't know they weren't going to come until Danny and I were sitting in the shop just a little while ago. We heard them laughing and talking about it. One of the boys said he was going to call and tell you he was a newspaper reporter after a story, just to see how you were taking it."

Marilyn's mom got deliberately to her feet, took two or three paces toward the kitchen, then turned to face Kay.

"That, my dear," she said icily, "is a very likely story. I want you to know that those young people who were invited to our party tonight are the children of very dear friends of mine. Even if they felt like doing something as rude as that they would never –."

At that instant the phone rang. Mrs. Forester stopped short. For a split instant a look of fright flickered in her eyes.

"I'll answer it, Mom," Marilyn said.

"I'll answer it myself," Mrs. Forester snapped.

The door chime sounded just then.

"That's probably Danny," Kay put in.

Marilyn let the Orlis boy in while her mom went to the telephone.

Mrs. Forester stood for a long while on the phone. "No," she said shortly, "I have no statement for the press about our party this evening. No, you may not come up with a photographer!" She hung up and for almost a minute stood there, bracing herself on a chair for support. Her breath was coming in long, tearing gasps. At last she turned and saw Danny.

"Good evening, Mrs. Forester," he said, managing a smile.

She stared but did not speak to him. He coughed nervously and looked in bewilderment toward Marilyn and Kay.

"You may tell your friend, whoever he was," she said acidly, "that his joke wasn't funny at all."

Danny looked at her blankly and started to speak, but she cut him off with a sudden motion of her hand.

"I suppose you'll be saying that you know nothing about it," she went on. "Well, if that will make you any happier, just go right ahead and blame it on the children of my friends."

"I don't think I know what you're talking about, Mrs. Forester," Danny told her.

"Mom seems to think you and Kay and – and the others caused the kids not to come to the party tonight, Danny," Marilyn explained. "She thinks you had one of the guys call and pretend to be a reporter."

"We didn't," the Orlis boy tried to assure her. "We heard them talking about it, but we didn't have anything to do with it."

Marilyn's mom chose to ignore their protests of innocence.

"For all of your so-called testimonies," she said angrily, "and this boasting about being Christian, you certainly have a very warped sense of humor."

Marilyn stared at her mom as though she could scarcely believe what she was hearing. Once or twice she started to speak, but she stopped uncertainly.

"I'm going up to bed, Marilyn," Mrs. Forester

announced. "You may feed your friends some of my sandwiches if you like. I want them to know that we are still kindly and Christian in our attitude toward them!"

The older woman took two or three steps toward the staircase, staggered uncertainly, and started to sag to the floor.

"Mom!" Marilyn cried out, running toward her. "Mom!"

Mrs. Forester moaned piteously and crumpled to the rug.

Danny and Kay rushed to her side. Marilyn had already reached her and was kneeling at her head, tears streaming down her face. Danny felt Mrs. Forester's pulse.

"Her heart seems to be strong enough," he said. "Her pulse is good."

"This is exactly what happened the other time," Marilyn exclaimed, her voice revealing her fright. "She was walking toward the stairs when she collapsed."

"Perhaps she's just fainted," Kay said evenly. The missionary's daughter had seen a great many accidents and much illness in her years on the mission field in Mexico with her mom. "Why don't you call the doctor?"

As Marilyn started to get to her feet, her mom stirred slightly, and her eyelids flickered.

"Mom!" Marilyn said tensely. She grasped Mrs. Forester by the shoulders with trembling hands.

Slowly her mom opened her eyes and shook her head. "No," she managed as though with a great deal of effort, "don't call Dr. Benton, Marilyn."

"But we've got to," the girl protested.

Her mom shook her head again. "I'll be all right," she quavered. "Don't mind me."

Danny and Kay looked at one another quizzically.

Mr. Forester came home just then, and Danny helped him get Marilyn's mom upstairs to bed.

"I'll call Dr. Benton and check with him," Harold Forester explained, "but I'm sure she'll be all right."

"I certainly hope so."

"And don't be too disturbed about what Mrs. Forester said," Marilyn's dad continued. "When she gets upset, she sometimes says things she doesn't mean." He smiled warmly. "I still want you to feel like coming over to the recreation room any time. We fixed that room for you, you know."

Kay and Danny didn't say much to each other on the way home that evening. They didn't feel like it.

CHAPTER 8

A MOM'S CONCERN

The evening before the youth group party at the church, Karen went into the living room where her mom was knitting.

"Well," Mrs. Meyer said, smiling, "is your dress ironed for the party tomorrow night?"

"Yes, Mom, it's all ready, but would you show me how to put up my hair tonight? I could do it myself, but I want it to look especially nice for tomorrow evening."

The older woman put aside her knitting. "Of course, I will," she answered, getting to her feet. "It isn't every night that a girl has her first date."

They brushed Karen's hair and Mrs. Meyer began to put it up with bobby pins.

"I can remember when I had my first date, Karen," her mom began.

"Did you feel all excited and scared at the same time, Mom?" Karen asked.

"I had butterflies in my stomach for a week."

The girl smiled. For some reason she felt a closeness to her mom now that she hadn't known for a long while. "Did you, really? I thought I was the only one who felt that way."

"I'm glad you've chosen a fine Christian boy, Karen," her mom went on, pinning a curl on her daughter's forehead. "Not that I think you ought to be in a relationship with Tom or anything like that. I want you to go out with different Christian boys. But it's so important that you always go out with Christians, Karen."

"Thanks, Mom, I will try to follow your advice."

All the next day Karen was so excited thinking about the party that she could not keep her mind on her studies.

After dinner Mrs. Meyer helped Karen get dressed, and a few minutes before 7:30, Tom rang the bell. Karen brought him in and introduced her parents. They liked him immediately and felt assured that Karen would be in good hands.

After they left, Mr. and Mrs. Meyer sat talking in the kitchen with the Bible on the table between them.

"I was so glad that Karen came to talk to me about her first date, John," Mrs. Meyer said. "It gave me an opportunity to say some things to her that I've wanted to say for a long while."

"I think that's fine," her husband answered. "But are you sure you went far enough? You know, when a young girl gets to her age, or even before, she has questions about a lot of things that she is going to have answered one way or another. She can get the information from home where she will learn these things in all their purity, or on the street, where it's cheap and vulgar."

"I wanted to talk to her a little more, John," Mrs. Meyer went on, "but frankly I felt so self-conscious talking to her."

"You shouldn't feel that way, dear," he said. "You should talk to her as soon as you can. If you avoid the subject once or twice, she may not come to you again."

Mr. Meyer went down to the store to work on the books, and Mrs. Meyer was sitting alone in the kitchen when her daughter came rushing in after the party.

"Oh, Mom," she exclaimed, "I had the most wonderful evening! Tommy and I went to the party at the church and had the most fun and – and then we went down to the shop for a soda." Her eyes were starry in her happiness. "And, Mom, he asked me if he could take me to another party some time."

"That's fine, honey."

Karen sat down across the table from her. "It was the most fun."

"I knew it would be," Mrs. Meyer smiled.

"And, Mom, Tommy has the same ideas about kissing and – and things like that, that you were telling me," she continued. "He said that he wouldn't want to kiss a girl – that he – that he didn't trust himself." The color came up into her cheeks a little.

"Tommy is a very wise young man."

There was a long silence.

"This probably sounds silly to you, Mom," Karen said at last. "But – but what did Tommy mean by that?"

The older woman was silent for a moment or two.

"I want to talk to you about that, dear," she began. "Your dad and I discussed this very thing last night. You know, God made man and woman for each other."

As she talked, her daughter moved closer to her, her big blue eyes growing serious. Now and then she stopped her mom and asked a question. Mrs. Meyer tried as best she could to answer. When at last she had finished, Karen looked up at her.

"You know, Mom," she said, "I've wondered and wondered about some of those things. I've heard the kids talk sometimes, but they made it sound so evil and – and dirty. It's so much different when you explain it. It's really something that's holy and sacred, isn't it?"

Mrs. Meyer nodded. "That's exactly right, Karen. It's a shame that so many young people get the wrong impression."

Karen got up and, walking around the table, put her arm on her mom's shoulder.

"I'm so glad that you talked to me, Mom."

Her mom reached up and took her hand in hers. "I'm glad I did too, Karen."

The next morning at breakfast Kirk glanced at Karen and began to grin.

"Do you know what I saw last night, Danny?" he asked.

"Now, Kirk," Karen warned.

"I saw Tommy Bailey and Karen walking down the street together. You should've seen them."

"Kirk!" The color came up in Karen's face. "You be quiet!"

"Well, I did! They went into the shop and sat down together in a booth. Karen just sat there looking at him all the time, just like she'd never seen a boy before. And he's got pimples on his face and everything."

Karen was blushing furiously.

"He has not!" Karen snapped. "Wait until I get hold of you."

"Now, Kirk," Mrs. Meyer said once more, "I don't want to hear any more of that. Karen, don't pay any attention to him."

Kirk started to speak, but a warning glance from Mr. Meyer caused him to stop abruptly. Karen looked up at her mom and smiled gratefully. It seemed there was a new bond of warmth, friendship, and understanding between them.

* * * *

Danny Orlis went out for baseball practice that evening after school. It was still cold and blustery, so Coach Collins contented himself with having the team warm up in the gym, going through strengthening exercises and tossing a ball about. The session was over earlier than usual. When Danny got home, Mrs. Meyer was still uptown. Roxie was sitting in the living room.

"Hi, Roxie."

"Hello, Danny."

He came over to where she was sitting. "What's the matter? You've been crying."

"I – I'm just not going back to that General Science class again, Danny."

"Why, what happened?" He sat beside her. "What's wrong?"

"I'm not going back there, Danny," she repeated firmly. "I'm not going to sit in class and listen to Mr. Clark make fun of the Bible and tell us that we don't even know that there is a God and things like that. I'm not going to do it!"

CHAPTER 9

A PASTOR'S INTEREST

Danny Orlis moved closer to his young sister.

"Now, Roxie," he said gently, "start from the beginning and tell me what this is all about."

She wiped at her eyes and sniffled a little.

"That Mr. Clark!" she blurted. "He started talking about the Bible this afternoon. He said some terrible things."

Danny nodded understandingly.

"He tried to tell us that the Bible isn't true. The way he talks, the story of creation is just a – well, he called it an old wives' tale. When I told him I believed the Bible, he started to make fun of me." She paused. "It was awful."

"I should have warned you about some of the teaching you were apt to get. It's the sort of thing many science classes all across the country are getting."

"He even said that we – we don't even know for sure that there is a God," Roxie said.

"But we know there is. We know that there is a God and that He sent His Son Jesus Christ to this earth to die on the cross and rise again so that we could be saved. And we know that He gave us His Book to tell us about Himself and how to live."

"Mr. Clark said that science has proved the Bible isn't true. He said that it's been proved we evolved from animals or something."

"We know that true science doesn't contradict the Bible," Danny said. "This evolution business he's been talking about isn't a proved fact. It's only a theory. I had a teacher once who told me there are just about as many theories of evolution as there are scientists who believe in it. And every one of these theories contradicts the others."

Roxie had dried her eyes by this time and was sitting beside her older brother, listening intently.

"There's another thing," the Orlis boy continued. "The last of the Bible was written more than nineteen hundred years ago, and we're still using the very same Bible. Do you know that science books five or ten years old aren't any good at all? Scientists are changing their minds all the time. So even the textbooks they write have to be thrown away every few years."

Danny talked with Roxie for a long while about evolution and science and the Word of God.

"I didn't really believe what he was saying, Danny," she said when he finished. "It was just that I had never heard anything like it before, and it made me so angry to have him laugh at me as he did."

Danny nodded sympathetically.

"Wait until I get back to school tomorrow," Roxie said with determination. "I'm really going to tell him what I think."

"Now, Roxie," Danny cautioned, "you want to be very careful what you say to Mr. Clark. Even though he talked to you the way he did, he's your teacher. He is in charge of your General Science class and entitled to your respect. So when you talk to him about anything, don't lose your temper or be disrespectful."

"All he did this afternoon was make fun of me," she protested.

"You're a Christian, don't forget that," Danny told her simply. "I know it will be hard, but that's why it is all the more important to act like one."

For a long while after Roxie had gone up to her room to study, Danny sat on the living room couch, staring at the floor. It was going to be hard for Roxie in General Science, terribly hard. He got up and started up the stairs to his room. That was just one more thing he'd have to pray about.

* * * *

Most of the kids at youth group were planning to attend the Bible Institute at Cedarton. Some of them had already been accepted. Others had just filed their applications. Interest was running high.

It was on a Thursday night following youth group that Pastor Arnold came up to Marilyn. "I suppose you're going to the Bible Institute with the rest of the young people," he said pleasantly.

The smile left her face.

"I'm not sure," she told him. "You see. Mom wants me to go to the university where she and Dad went."

"Oh," the pastor replied, "I've been hoping you would be able to go to the Institute too! It's going to be a wonderful place to get good, solid Bible training."

He talked with her further about the situation, and the following afternoon he and his wife went to call on Mrs. Forester.

"And so," he concluded, "we thought we would talk with you about letting Marilyn attend the Bible Institute. She needs the fellowship of Christian friends and the Bible teaching she would get here. It's just the thing to ground her in the faith."

There was a short silence.

"My only concern," Mrs. Forester said frigidly, her pale blue eyes staring at her visitors, "is that Marilyn do what is best for her and, frankly, I'm not at all sure that a Bible Institute is the best for her. She's so young, Mr. Arnold, and so – so religious. She needs the guidance of older, more mature judgment, don't you think?"

"I think," he replied evenly, "that she needs exactly what the Bible Institute will be able to give her. Two years of training in the Scriptures would give her a sound foundation for her faith. She would then be able to withstand the temptations and false teachings that so often crop up at a secular school and could still benefit from their excellent facilities."

"Now, don't misunderstand me," Mrs. Forester countered. "I have no objection to Marilyn attending the Bible Institute. The only thing her father and I insist on is that she do what is best for her." She paused and huge, luminous tears appeared in her eyes. She sniffled audibly and, with an elaborate flourish, took a tissue and dabbed at her eyes. "We want Marilyn to be happy more than anything else in the world. If she wants to go to the Bible Institute, or whatever you call it, then that's where we are going to insist that she go, regardless of our own wishes in the matter."

"I'm so glad you feel that way, Mrs. Forester," the pastor answered. "Marilyn is a lovely Christian girl. I know you will never regret making it possible for her to attend the Institute where her faith and knowledge of the Scriptures will be strengthened."

* * * *

From that moment on, Mrs. Forester's attitude toward the Christian kids changed abruptly. For the past several weeks she had been kind and gracious to them, going out of her way to fix snacks or dessert whenever they were congregated in the basement.

Now and then she went down to talk with them. And no one ever left that she didn't follow to the door and urge them to come back.

Now, all that was over. She said nothing to them when Danny and Kay and the others came to have a committee meeting or just to enjoy the recreation room. She still allowed Marilyn to fix food and invite her friends as often as she wished, but she made no effort to hide her disgust. She glared at them over her magazine as they came into the house. And on more than one occasion she got up and left the room to avoid having to talk with them.

"I don't know why that minister of yours thought it was any of his business," she told her daughter, angrily. "But it's as I told him. What your father and I want more than anything else is to see you happy. And," she shrugged her shoulders expressively, "if going to that Bible Institute is what it takes to make you happy, then that's what I want for you."

Marilyn kissed her impulsively.

"You're a darling, Mom!"

Mrs. Forester smiled.

"I'm glad you're happy, dear. That's all that matters. It doesn't make any difference what I want, just so long as you're happy."

"Is – is it all right if I apply for entrance to the Institute after school tomorrow?" she asked.

The older woman swallowed hard. "Why don't you wait until Dad gets home before you do that? He ought to be back in two or three days."

Mr. Forester got through with his business in Chicago sooner than he had expected and came home on the train the following afternoon. As soon as he stepped into the house his wife told him about the minister's visit and what Marilyn wished to do.

"Why, I think that's fine, Carrie. She's young. She's got plenty of time to go to the Bible Institute for a couple of years and still go down to the U and get her degree."

"You mean you actually want her to go out here to school with these – these fanatics?"

"I don't know of anything that would make me happier."

Tears flooded Mrs. Forester's eyes. "I might have known that you would be against me too." Her thin voice trembled. "I should have known you'd stick up for her, you and that Mr. Arnold."

"Just wait, Carrie," he told her. "When you see what the Bible Institute is and how much it will help Marilyn, you'll be really thankful that she is going there." He took off his coat and hung it in the hall closet.

His wife let a big tear roll, unheeded, down her cheek.

"I don't know why that preacher figured it was any of his business," she retorted angrily. "Nobody asked him to come over here, sticking his nose into our affair. That religion Marilyn's so fanatical about has given us enough trouble."

"I'm glad that Pastor Arnold is concerned enough about the young people to care where they go to school," Harold Forester answered. "This Bible school is going to be good for Marilyn. I checked into it the other day. They've got a fine staff of teachers, fine facilities, and as good a library as any school of its size in the country. She'll get a good education there." He went over and put his arm around his wife. "Why don't we let her go to school here? It's what she wants."

Mrs. Forester gulped hard and bit her lower lip.

CHAPTER 10

AN UNUSUAL VISIT

Marilyn Forester talked with her mom once more about going to Bible school.

"Are you sure that's what you wish to do?" Mrs. Forester asked.

"More than anything in the world," Marilyn told her. "All the kids I hang out with will be there. I want to go to the university, but I want to get some Bible training first."

The older woman walked over to the couch and sat down, wearily, as though her daughter's announcement had suddenly drained all the strength from her.

"Well," she said, "if that's what you want – if that's your wish, I'm not going to say another word. You know what I want you to do. You know how I've worked and waited and planned for the day when you would take your position among the children of my friends. I've so wanted you to take your rightful place in my sorority at the U. But you aren't content to do what I want you to do, so I've said all I'm going to. You do as you please."

"I know you'll never be sorry that I decided to go to the Institute. In a couple of years, if you still want me to go to the U, I'll be glad to go."

The next evening after school Marilyn went out to the Institute and applied for entrance. When she came back, she talked with her mom about it.

"I want to hear no more about it," Mrs. Forester retorted.

The smile left Marilyn's face.

Mrs. Forester did not sleep that night or the next. What if Marilyn should start to date one of those destitute young missionaries? What if she fell in love with one of those boys and wanted to marry him? The older woman sat up in bed, fear squeezing her heart. She couldn't have Marilyn living a life of poverty! She just couldn't! Something would have to be done!

All the next morning she could think of nothing else. It was bad enough having Marilyn spend two years at a Bible Institute, where her whole life was apt to be warped and twisted worse than it was already. What was worse, it was quite possible that she might meet one of those young men and fall in love with him. That would ruin everything!

Mrs. Forester was sitting in the living room when she realized what she had to do. She got up quickly and glanced at her watch. There wasn't time before lunch to go out and see the president at the Bible Institute. She would go and see him as soon as Marilyn had gone back to school.

She bustled about the kitchen cooking lunch, humming a little tune, and smiling inwardly. Why hadn't she thought of that before?

As soon as her daughter was safely back in school, Mrs. Forester got out her car and drove to the Bible Institute on the edge of town. President Neilsen showed her into his office.

"Yes," he said, thumbing through some of the papers on his desk, "we have Marilyn's application here. We received some very good recommendations for her. She's the kind of a girl we like to have. She'll be a credit to our school."

"That, Dr. Neilsen," Mrs. Forester began, "is what I came to talk with you about." Her face was white and drawn and her hands were working nervously. "I just don't know how to tell you this, but – but in spite of those recommendations I couldn't, in honesty, have Marilyn attend here unless you knew the truth."

Dr. Neilsen took off his glasses and peered intently at her. "Just what do you mean?"

Mrs. Forester swallowed hard and let a tear escape her eyelid and trickle down her powderless cheeks. "You'll never know how hard this is," she said, "or how I've tortured myself before deciding to come to you. But Marilyn isn't what she seems to be."

"Do you feel as though you can tell me any more?" he asked gently.

Mrs. Forester sniffled and wiped at the tears again. Without makeup and in a faded, straight- lined dress she looked old and careworn. "I would rather not do that, Dr. Neilsen," she managed. "I will tell you, however, that Marilyn is living a very worldly life. Why, only last fall, she put on one of the biggest dances the country club has ever seen. And last week she invited a group of rough kids for a party right at our house." Mrs. Forester paused momentarily, wiping away another tear.

The school president picked up a pencil from his desk and studied it for a moment or two. "I know how hard this must be for you, Mrs. Forester," he said at last. "It takes real Christian grace for a mom to do something like this."

"But what will you do about her application?" she asked.

"If it were anyone except you," he said, "I'd dismiss it by saying that the recommendations we got far outweigh the testimony of one person. But a girl's mom should know more about her than anyone else."

Relief was evident in Mrs. Forester's face. "And – and you won't say anything to anybody about it, will you?" she asked. "I'm afraid that others wouldn't understand."

"You can rest assured that I'll treat this visit with complete confidence," the president told her.

A DAD'S CONCERN

The first of the week Danny and Kay and the others received notices of their acceptance to the Bible Institute.

"I thought I'd get mine too," Marilyn said, as Kay showed her the letter she had received. "But I suppose it will be coming along in a few days. I did get my application in a little late."

"You won't have to worry about making it as I did," one of the girls put in. "You could get into any school in the country with your grades."

"I hope I don't have any trouble," Marilyn answered.

Tim began to come back to Sunday school and church and youth group, and he and Marilyn started dating occasionally again. He took her to a party at church and one at school. On two or three occasions he came over to play ping pong or some other game.

"I almost wish I were going to Bible school with

everyone else," he said, as half the youth group sat talking. "It sounds as though you are going to have a lot of fun."

"I think they've got room for you out there too," Danny told him.

"I've got to go to Crestwood if I go to school at all. I won't have money enough to swing it if I don't take advantage of that scholarship."

"And the new car," somebody else said.

"That car didn't have very much to do with it," Tim replied seriously. "I've decided that I'm going to make my time down there really count for God. I'm going to live so that my life will be a real testimony on the campus. And I'm not going to be afraid to speak about Christian things to the guys I'll be playing football with. I'm going to make my stay at Crestwood worthwhile."

"I'm glad to hear you say that," Danny said. "I know there are some Christians who are able to do just that. But the pressure is going to be awfully strong."

Danger signals flashed in Tim's eyes. "I thought we went all over that," he retorted.

"I'm sorry, Tim," the Orlis boy replied. "And another thing, I'm going to withdraw my name from that silly popularity contest. I mean that."

Tim looked at his friend. First, he seemed deadly serious, then his face broke into a good-natured grin as he said, "I'm with you. Let's be unpopular!"

* * * *

Roxie had more trouble in General Science as the days went by. Mr. Clark seemed to enjoy making fun of her faith and her belief in the Bible's story of creation.

He would call on her now and again with caustic, bitter questions. However, she remembered what Danny had told her and treated him respectfully. When it came to making out her daily paper she would write, "The book said," and then would give the book's answer. That showed she had studied her lesson and knew what the book answer was, even though she didn't believe it herself.

"Back in the dark ages," the teacher began one afternoon, "the learned men of the day believed what the Bible said. Because they didn't know any better they accepted it as truth. In these enlightened times we know a great deal more about such matters. We know, for example, that all life came into being and developed from a simple one-celled animal. We know that man is the highest creature on the evolutionary ladder and that he still bears some of the character-istics of his earlier ancestors."

Roxie began to squirm.

"Of course," he said, looking down at her once more, "I know that what I am saying is a shock to at least one in the class." He picked up a ruler and began to tap softly on his desk. "I'd like to have a little debate in this class next week. I'd like to see just what arguments can be presented for the Bible's story of creation." He got up and walked to one corner of the room where he turned to face the class. "I think we're going to have a debate on the subject, 'Resolved: that man evolved from a simple, one-celled animal.'"

Roxie felt her cheeks go white. She cringed as two or three kids who sat in front of her turned around and snickered.

"Be thinking about this subject and do a little research on it over the weekend," the teacher went on. "We're going to pick out our debaters on Monday. Next Friday, instead of a regular class period, we'll have a debate."

He was talking to all the class, although he was looking directly at Roxie.

"But, Danny," she explained after supper that evening, "I just know that he's going to expect me to be on the other side of that question. He's going to want me to be on the affirmative and give arguments that are supposed to prove the Bible is not true."

For a moment or two the Orlis boy said nothing.

"And I can't do it, Danny!" she continued. "I just can't."

"You know, Roxie," her older brother said, "this is something we ought to pray about. We'll take the matter to the Lord and leave it there. He can work it out for you."

"But how?" she asked.

"That's a question God will have to answer for you, Roxie."

Roxie looked up at him.

"I'm so glad that I have you to talk with, Danny," she said. "I feel better about it already."

"I'll be praying about it too," he assured her.

Danny went out to a youth group committee meeting that evening and came in shortly before midnight. Mr. and Mrs. Meyer were sitting in the living room.

"Oh," Mr. Meyer said as the Orlis boy came in, "I thought you were Karen!"

"Isn't she home yet?" Danny asked.

Mr. Meyer shook his head.

"The last two or three times she's had dates, she's been staying out a little later each time," he explained. "Now it's almost two hours past the time we've asked her to be in, and she's still not here."

Danny started up the stairs just as the door opened and Karen came in. He would have gone on, but Mr. Meyer asked him to wait.

"Are you still up?" Karen asked her parents, taking off her coat and hanging it in the hall closet.

"Yes," Mr. Meyer said sternly, "we're still up. Do you know what time it is, young lady?"

A guilty look came across her face. "It – it isn't late, is it?"

"Take a look at the clock. We've asked you to be in by 10 o'clock, and it's almost 12. Where have you been, and what have you been doing?"

"Oh," she said, trying to sound casual, "we just

walked home after the party at school and got to talking in the shop."

"The shop closes at 10 o'clock," Mrs. Meyer put in.

"Then we walked around awhile."

"This can't happen again," Mr. Meyer told her. "And to help you remember the next time, I don't think you'd better have any more dates for a month."

"A – a whole month?"

"That's right," he said sternly. "And from now on you are to be in by 10 o'clock unless you're at some school or church party and have talked with us about it first."

Karen burst into tears and fled upstairs. Danny would have followed her, but Mr. Meyer called to him.

"Danny," he said, "I'd like to talk with you for a minute."

"Sure thing," the Orlis boy answered. He went over to the couch and sat down.

"I've been wanting to talk with you about getting in a little earlier, Danny," Mr. Meyer told him. "I talked with Karen about this thing a few days ago, and she used you as an example. She said that you stayed out late, so she ought to be able to do the same."

"I'm sorry, Mr. Meyer," Danny told him. "I hadn't really thought anything about it."

"I know you haven't. And I haven't said anything to you about it before. But we really would appreciate it a great deal if you would try to get in a little earlier. The kids know that you have a strong Christian testimony, and they look to you for guidance. When they see that you are out late at night, they feel that it's an excuse for them to be out too."

"I certainly had never thought of it that way," Danny answered. "What time do you think I ought to be in?"

"I believe that if you were in by 10:30 or 11 o'clock it would be all right," Mr. Meyer said. "Karen would know that you would have to have a little extra time to get home after you had taken your girl home. And I'm sure the parents of the girl you happen to date would appreciate it a great deal if you made a practice of bringing their daughter home by 10 o'clock, the same as we are expecting of Karen."

* * * *

Danny Orlis walked home with Marilyn the next evening after youth group. They were planning to have a committee meeting and play a little ping pong afterward.

"I'm so glad that Mom decided I could go to Bible school," Marilyn said. "I've prayed and prayed about it. For the longest time it looked as though she were going to make me go to the university. All of a sudden she changed her mind and said it would be all right for me to enroll out here."

"That's great."

"Dad and I have been praying every night and every morning since Dad accepted Christ that Mom would also trust Jesus as her Savior. Whenever I get my application accepted at Bible school, I'm going to talk with her about the Lord again. I just know she's going to come through this time."

"Just the other day Tim told me the same thing about his mom, Marilyn," the Orlis boy said.

She stopped and turned to face him. "Wouldn't it be wonderful if they would both accept Christ as Savior?"

When they entered the house Mrs. Forester got up hurriedly and came to meet them.

"Well, hello there, young man," she beamed. "It's been so long since you've been over to see Marilyn."

"Danny was here last Saturday night, Mom," Marilyn said. "Don't you remember?"

"I guess it just seems like a long while," Mrs. Forester continued. "You two children go down to the basement and have a good time. I've got a cake in the oven that I'll share with you after a while."

Marilyn and the Orlis boy had started down the stairs when her mom came hurrying after her. "I forgot to give you this letter, my dear. It was in the post office box when I got the mail this evening."

Marilyn took the letter eagerly. "Why, it's from the Bible Institute," she said. "It must be my acceptance."

Excitedly she tore open the envelope and unfolded the letter. Her cheeks went ashen and her lips trembled uncertainly.

"What's the matter?" Danny asked.

"I – I don't know."

"Is something wrong, Marilyn?" Danny asked her.

"It's a letter from Dr. Neilsen," she said, her voice sounding dull and far away. "They are rejecting my application."

CHAPTER 12

AN UNEXPECTED BLOW

A long, breathless hush settled over the Forester living room. Marilyn's shoulders trembled. She moved dazedly across the room and sank to the couch. Her mom went over and put her arm about her shoulder.

"It can't be true, Marilyn. They can't do that to you."

"I can't understand it," Marilyn said. "All the other kids were accepted, and some of them had lower grades than I had. I can't understand it."

"Perhaps they made a mistake, Marilyn," Danny told her. "You've been on the honor roll for the past two years, so it couldn't be your grades. And I know there isn't anything wrong with your Christian testimony. Perhaps they got your records mixed with those of somebody else."

"I'm so sorry for you, my dear," Mrs. Forester continued soothingly. "I'm terribly sorry that something like this had to happen to hurt my little girl."

Marilyn started to speak, then choked suddenly.

"There now, darling," her mom said, "don't feel so bad." She dabbed at her daughter's eyes with clumsy tenderness. "They aren't worth shedding tears over. This is the sort of thing I've been afraid would happen. This is what you can expect when you associate with such fanatics."

"But they aren't fanatics, Mom," she protested. "They're good, sincere Christians who are doing the best they can to run a Christian school."

"Do you think such good Christians would treat an innocent girl like you the way they have?" Mrs. Forester asked pointedly.

Danny Orlis shifted nervously from one foot to the other. Marilyn's mom looked up at him, her eyes snapping.

"I think you had better leave now, young man," she said curtly. "It's as likely as not that you had something to do with this."

"Don't go, Danny," Marilyn said quickly. "I've got to have somebody to talk to."

But her mom shook her head. "The less you have to do with people like him the better. If you hadn't gone overboard on this religion stuff you wouldn't be so badly hurt now. Your father and I both went to the U. They would welcome you."

* * * *

Danny Orlis had a difficult time getting to sleep that night. Of all the girls in the youth group, aside from Kay, he would have been the most surprised to learn that Marilyn's application had been rejected.

The next morning he called Kay and walked to school with her. She was stunned to learn about Marilyn.

"But there must be a mistake," she said firmly. "Dr. Neilsen surely wouldn't reject Marilyn if he had all the facts and contacted the people who knew her."

"Do you suppose we could talk to Marilyn and get her to go with us to talk to him?" Danny asked.

But Marilyn would not listen to it.

"No," she said sharply when Danny and Kay asked her about it that afternoon. "They don't want me out there; they've told me that. I'm not going out and beg them. I told Mom this morning that I've decided to apply at the U. That's what I should have done in the first place."

Kay called Marilyn the following Sunday morning and asked her to go to church and Sunday school with her, but she had an excuse.

"Besides," she said, "Mom asked me to go to church with her this morning. I want to talk with some of the kids who are planning on going to school at the university next fall. Mom thought that several of us ought to get together and go down to the sorority with her to spend a weekend."

"It wasn't only that she turned me down," Kay

told Danny dejectedly that afternoon. "It was the way she did it, as though she just didn't care anymore."

"It was an awfully hard blow for her," Danny said. "Poor kid."

* * * *

The next day in General Science class Mr. Clark made assignments for the coming debate.

"I presume," he began, "that you would like to be on the negative side of this proposition, Roxie. Is that right?"

"I want to be on the side that defends the Bible."

Two or three guys snickered loudly.

"Now," he continued, "who wants to debate with her?"

Not a hand went up.

"Isn't there anyone else in our class who believes the Bible account of creation?" Mr. Clark smirked.

Roxie looked around. Again, there were no hands up.

"It looks as though you're slightly outnumbered," he told her. "I'll have to draft somebody to be with you, unless you want to default right now?"

She shook her head.

He looked up one row and down the other. Finally he said, "All right, Don Edwards, I want you to debate with Roxie."

"Aw," Don protested, color tinting his cheeks, "can't you find somebody else?"

"You will debate with Roxie," the teacher repeated. "You will have until Friday to prepare your arguments."

He appointed a team to take the affirmative, and then the class was dismissed.

"I think Danny would help us, Don," Roxie said, talking with her partner after class.

"He'll have to. I don't know anything about the Bible. The fact is, I'd rather have been on the other side."

Don Edwards came over to the Meyers' house that evening, and Danny helped him and Roxie get material together to study. He found three or four good books and a number of articles.

"This gets me," the younger boy said, as Danny showed them the material be had on the subject. "I didn't know that there was any real evidence to help prove that the Bible is true."

"I'm afraid there are a lot of people who think that," Danny told him. "But the truth of the matter is that an increasing number of scientists are coming to accept the Bible's position. Take the matter of creation for example. There must be dozens of scientific theories about it, but the one theory which has the most evidence behind it is the one which says that all the stars, the sun, and the earth were created at once. Some of the scientists who believe that don't accept the Bible, that's true, but their theory is exactly the same as the Bible's account of creation."

Danny went on to tell the younger boy more of what

the Word of God had to say. Don's eyes widened as he sat forward on the edge of the seat, listening intently.

"I certainly didn't know that the Bible told all those things," he said at last.

"The Bible isn't a science book," Danny said, "but we can be sure of this much – whenever the Bible mentions science, what it has to say on the subject is true."

The Orlis boy went on to explain the plan of salvation, how the Lord Jesus Christ had come to earth to live a sinless life; how He was crucified, buried, and rose again on the third day so that all those who believed on Him might have eternal life. Don Edwards swallowed hard and squirmed uneasily. As soon as Danny finished, he got to his feet.

"I – I've got to be going," he said lamely, edging toward the door. "Thanks, Danny. Thanks a lot."

"Do you suppose we can get together again tomorrow night, Don?" Roxie asked him. "We've got a lot of work to do if we're going to win this debate."

For an instant or two he looked over at Danny, hesitating.

"Will you be here, Danny?" he asked.

"I've got to go to youth group for a short meeting," the young woodsman told him. "But I'll certainly help all I can. Perhaps I can bring Kay over tomorrow night. She's a genius on this stuff."

"That will be fine," Roxie dimpled. When her debating companion was gone, she came back into the living room where Danny was sitting. "Danny," she asked, "would you pray for us in this debate? I know that unless God helps us, we won't be able to win. And, Danny, we've just got to! We might never be able to reach any of those kids for Christ if we don't."

The youth group meeting came and went. Kay made a special effort to get Marilyn to come out for it, but the heartbroken girl refused.

"I'm awfully sorry, Kay," she said over the phone, "but I won't be able to make it tonight. I've got a terrible headache."

"Oh," the missionary's daughter answered, "that's too bad!"

There was a long silence.

"I shouldn't have said that, Kay," Marilyn apologized. "I do have a little headache, but that isn't the real reason I'm not going. I can't bring myself to face the rest of the group and have to listen to them talk about going to Bible school."

When her dad came home from his trip East, Marilyn was lying on the couch, her eyes red and swollen. Her mom had gone to a committee meeting, and Marilyn was alone.

"Why, Marilyn," her dad said as he came in the door, "I thought you'd be at youth group tonight."

She shook her head.

Her dad set down his suitcase and walked over to where she was lying.

"What's the matter, darling?"

For a moment she could not speak. He sat down

beside her and put his arm tenderly about her shoulder. "Tell me," he said softly, "what's wrong."

She swallowed hard. "It – it's the school," she blurted.

"Your mom and I settled that school business before I left. You don't have to go down to the U. You can go to the Bible school here if you wish."

"That's just it, Daddy," she exclaimed. "I can't go to the Bible school here. They – they rejected my application."

Harold Forester stared at his daughter.

"Rejected! But why?" he asked. "What happened?"

"I don't know. I got a letter from Dr. Neilsen."

"There must be some mistake."

At that instant Mrs. Forester came in.

"Carrie," Harold said to his wife, "why didn't you tell me the Bible school had rejected Marilyn's application when I called yesterday?"

She flushed slightly and turned to hang up her coat. "I didn't want to bother you, Harold. I knew it would be a shock to you."

Mr. Forester crossed the room. "I can't understand it. I just can't understand it."

CHAPTER 13

ALL HANDS UP!

That evening after Marilyn had gone to bed, Mr. and Mrs. Forester sat together in the living room of their beautiful home.

"Marilyn's grades have always been among the best," Harold Forester said, "and her conduct and testimony have been above reproach for the past year or so. I can't understand why Dr. Neilsen rejected her application."

"Oh, you know how some of those religious fanatics are," Carrie replied carelessly. "She could have said something to somebody or have done something he didn't approve of. There's no understanding people like that, or what they're going to do."

Marilyn's dad shook his head.

"Dr. Neilsen isn't that way. He spoke at our luncheon group just before I left for the East. He struck me as being a solid, sound-thinking individual. He isn't apt to make a decision like this unless he has a very good reason."

"It won't do any good for us to worry about it. She can get into the university and make a marvelous record. She'll show these religious fanatics that she's too good for their narrow little school."

"This is going to be a terrible blow for her. She didn't go to youth group tonight, and I've got a hunch that she wasn't in church or Sunday school last Sunday."

"If you ask me," Carrie Forester snapped, her temper rising, "Marilyn could do with a lot less of this religion. And so could you."

* * * *

All that week Danny Orlis continued to help Roxie and Don with their debate material. They copied quotations from outstanding authorities and the learned observations of many scientists to place alongside the Word of God.

Interest in the debate ran high. Mr. Clark spread the news of it among the other classes, and by the time Friday afternoon rolled around the whole school was talking about it.

"I'd certainly like to hear that debate this afternoon," Tim said to Roxie as he met her in the hall. "Danny tells me that you and Don have really been working."

"We've been working and praying too. At least I have."

"The whole youth group is praying for you, Roxie," he assured her.

"Thanks."

When Roxie finally got to the General Science room, she was surprised to see that Mr. Clark had made arrangements for all of those who had library that period to sit in on the debate. The room was jammed.

"You know the proposition we're debating," the teacher smiled, looking over at Roxie and Don. "Many of you have been doing a good deal of reading and thinking about it this week. I'm going to ask all of you to serve as judges. We're going to see how persuasive our debaters are this afternoon."

He paused significantly. Laughter rippled across the audience.

Don looked over at Roxie and smiled timidly.

"How many of you believe that man evolved from lower and more simple forms of life?" the teacher asked abruptly.

There was a little hesitation, and then, one after another, the hands began to go up. Mr. Clark smiled broadly.

"It looks almost unanimous," he observed. "Now, how many believe the Bible account of creation?"

Roxie's hand shot up instantly. Don looked over at her, and then back at the instructor. His face flushed as he timidly raised his hand just a little above his shoulder.

"Well, well, well!" Mr. Clark said. "It looks as though we've only got two people who believe the Bible story. And," he paused, his smile widening, "there seems to be a little doubt in the mind of one of those. I want you all to listen carefully. When the debate is over, we'll take another poll."

The first speaker for evolution built his case around the story of the various fossils which have been found in different kinds of rock.

Don countered with the story of creation which Danny had told him, going back to the authority from whom the Orlis boy had read his information.

The next speaker told of the various skulls and bones that anthropologists had discovered, both of which were supposed to prove that man at one time had a very different and very limited intelligence. He traced the theory of evolution from the one-celled amoeba, up through the fishes, reptiles, birds and animals. ". . . until finally," he concluded, "we have man as we know him today."

With the opening rebuttal Don quoted a report which stated that the Piltdown Man, long accepted by the scientists as positive evidence of evolution, was actually only a clever fake. He told of the Nebraska man that was reconstructed from a small piece of jawbone which had been discovered some thirty years before, and which, it later developed, was the jawbone of a prehistoric pig. He told of a skeleton in Colorado which had excited evolution-believing scientists. It was again held as proof of man's evolution, only to be later proved a skeleton of a monkey.

Roxie picked up where her companion left off, quoting authority after authority who had made exhaustive studies and findings, which tended to substantiate the Bible account. She called attention to the fact that nowhere in the world have successive layers of rock been found which contain fossils in the order which scientists claim that evolution followed. On the contrary, the archaeologists have been disturbed by the fact that in many places the rocks, which according to their theory should have been formed last, actually have been found on the bottom, or in the middle. She quoted the Bible too, calling attention to the fact that it has been unchanged some nineteen hundred years, while some scientific books ten or fifteen years old are considered obsolete and worthless.

The audience was listening intently, leaning forward and grasping every word. Mr. Clark scowled a little and, getting to his feet, strode across to the window and looked out until the debate was finally over.

"Well," he said, shuffling the papers on his desk, "that will be all for today."

"But you were going to take another vote, Mr. Clark," Don spoke quickly.

He looked at his watch. "I guess there is time. How many of you believe that man evolved from a lower, more simple form of life, the way all leading scientists believe?"

The class sat motionless. Only the hands of the two debaters who had defended the proposition still signified that they believed man had evolved from an animal.

The color came up in Mr. Clark's face. "I don't believe you understood me," he said. "How many of you believe that man evolved from a simple form of life?"

There was a stir in the class, but only the same two hands went up.

"Well," the teacher said, "it looks as though we had some good debaters on the negative this afternoon. How many of you believe that man was created by God just as he is today?"

Without a moment's hesitation every hand in the room went up, except those of the affirmative debaters and Mr. Clark. It was apparent to all present that the edge of the debate was in favor of the Christian students.

The teacher turned to Don and Roxie. "We'll have the same debate a week from today," he said. "Only this time we'll change sides. You two will take the affirmative."

The bell rang just then and class was dismissed. Roxie sat there, the color fading from her face. Finally, when the room was empty, she went up to the teacher's desk.

"Mr. Clark," she began hesitantly.

He looked up irritably.

"I can't be on the affirmative side of this debate," she said, trying hard to remain courteous and respectful. "I was speaking what I believed this afternoon. I can't get up next week and argue against the Word of God."

"Nonsense," Mr. Clark retorted.

He turned back to his work, but she still stood there.

"I can't do it, Mr. Clark," she went on. "I want to do every assignment you give me, but I just can't do this one."

"Do I take it," he began severely, looking up at her, "that you are deliberately disobeying me?"

"I don't want to," she told him. "It's like Danny said, that the least a student should do is to have the proper respect for his teacher. But I – I just can't debate against God."

The teacher stared at her. "I could flunk you for this."

She swallowed hard. "I know."

Then he smiled. "But I'm not going to. I admire your courage and your arguments."

* * * *

Back at the Forester home that Friday evening, Marilyn's dad laid aside his book.

"You know, Carrie," he said, after looking about to make sure that Marilyn was out of the rom, "I haven't been able to get Marilyn out of my mind all day."

"The best thing we can do now is to forget about it. She's reconciled to going to the U. It'll be the best for her anyway. She'll be with her own kind there."

"But it's so unlike Dr. Neilsen and so unlike Marilyn. Why on earth would any school reject her? It couldn't be for spiritual reasons. And I checked at the high school today and learned that she's in the upper twenty percent of her class. So they couldn't have rejected her on scholastic grounds."

"But they did reject her, my dear."

"I'm not satisfied. I'm going out and talk to Dr. Neilsen."

Mrs. Forrester's face blanched.

"I've worried about this thing long enough," he said. "I'm going to get to the bottom of it."

A strange, frightened look came into Carrie Forester's eyes. "Harold," she protested desperately, "don't."

He turned to face her.

"And why not? Why shouldn't I find out why my daughter's application was turned down?"

"It–it'll only make matters worse, Harold," she said desperately. "And there isn't any good that can come from it."

He walked past her and was getting his coat out of the hall closet.

She followed him, taking hold of his arm.

"Harold!"

He turned to face her. Her knees gave way, and she crumpled to the floor.

CHAPTER 14

"A TERRIBLE MISTAKE"

Harold Forester knelt quickly beside his wife.

"Carrie!" he exclaimed, feeling for her pulse. "Carrie!" Concern was in his voice.

Her eyes were tightly closed, and her arms and legs sprawled like those of a rag doll thrown carelessly aside. For an instant he couldn't catch her pulse, and his own heart skipped erratically. A thin line of sweat formed on his forehead and his hands were trembling.

"Carrie!"

Then his shaking fingers caught her pulse. He had been so sure it would be fast and fluttering that it startled him. It was firm and even, and as strong as his own. At first he thought he might be feeling his own pulse in his haste to catch hers. Her pulse was normal. He sighed audibly.

For the space of a heartbeat he thought he saw her eyelids quiver. Staring at her intently he saw it again, so faint and fast that he could not be sure. Then he saw her eyes open slowly, just a thin sliver, to close frantically when she saw that he was watching her.

Grasping her by the shoulders he shook her roughly. "Carrie!" he exclaimed. This time his voice was stern. "Carrie! Open your eyes!"

She did not move.

He shook her again. "If you won't wake up for me, perhaps you will for Doc Benton."

He got to his feet and picked up the telephone. As he dialed the first number she turned and raised on one elbow.

"Harold!"

He dialed the second digit without looking toward her.

"Harold!" she called loudly. "What are you doing?"

He set the phone down and turned to face her.

"All right," he said coldly, "suppose you tell me what this is all about?"

"I – I must have fainted," she said weakly. She held out a trembling hand, and he helped her to her feet and guided her over to the couch.

"I – I feel so funny, Harold." There was a tinge of desperation in her voice. "All of a sudden everything went black. I guess I've been so concerned about Marilyn's being rejected at the Bible Institute that I – that I –."

"That you what, Carrie?"

"That I overtaxed my heart."

"A while ago you said you didn't care about Marilyn's being rejected at the Bible school," he reminded her. "You said she could get into the university, and that was all that mattered."

"After all, a mom doesn't like to have her – her own daughter refused entrance to a school. Especially to a school with standards like they're supposed to have at the Bible Institute."

Harold Forester sat down across from his wife, still eying her intently.

"There are some things I've got to get straight. What happened just now, Carrie? And why did it happen?"

"I – I fainted," she answered. "At least that's what it must have been. Either that or my heart. You know how my heart has been lately with all this trouble about Marilyn and everything." She stopped, looking at him wistfully, but he neither spoke nor took his eyes from her.

"I came over to kiss you good-bye and all of a sudden everything went black. The next I knew you were on the telephone."

Harold Forester shook his head. "You'll have to do better than that, Carrie. I want the truth."

"But you believe me, don't you?" she begged. There was fright in her eyes.

"I wish I could," he told her. "But that wasn't a faint just now nor a heart attack."

He paused and took a deep breath. "I've wondered about these spells you've had from time to time before. They seemed to come in very handy as you tried to gain a point with Marilyn about her friends or her church or the school she chose."

She straightened indignantly. "I've never been so insulted in my life."

"The doctor hinted as much to me the last time we called him out. But this affair tonight was the giveaway, as far as I am concerned." He shook his head. "You weren't fainting, Carrie, you were faking – from start to finish. Your pulse was as regular and firm as mine, and I saw you open your eyes three different times to see how your act was going over." He took a deep breath. "Why?" he demanded.

There was no answer. By this time her face had become very pale. Her heavily powdered forehead was beaded with sweat and her lips were trembling.

"Were you trying to keep me from going out to the Bible Institute to talk with Dr. Neilsen?" he asked.

"Why would I care if you talked with Dr. Neilsen or whatever his name is. It's nothing to me."

"That's exactly what I want to find out."

For two full minutes he sat there, staring at her. She wiped at her forehead with her hands and sniffled to keep back the tears.

"You don't trust me. You don't believe what I tell you. That's the cruelest thing you've ever said to me."

Mr. Forester got to his feet and took a step toward his wife, towering over her.

"Should I believe you?" he asked. "Should I?"

She began to wipe at her eyes.

"I'm going out to see Dr. Neilsen now, Carrie," he said. "But I want to talk with you about this whole affair when I get back."

"No!" she exclaimed quickly, her eyes widening.

"No, what?"

"You can't go out there and talk to that – that Dr. Neilsen," she quavered.

Harold Forester laid his coat aside deliberately and came back to where his wife was seated.

"I think I'm beginning to understand," he said at last. "You were out to see Dr. Neilsen while I was gone, weren't you?"

She started to sniffle again.

"I – I only did it for Marilyn's own good. I only did it for her."

Harold Forester's voice was harsh.

"I think you had better start from the beginning, Carrie," he said, "and tell me everything. This time I'm going to hear the truth!"

Hesitantly, tearfully, Mrs. Forester told him how she had felt about Marilyn's going to the Bible Institute. She told him how worried she had been about the fact that Marilyn would likely meet a young, would-be preacher and fall in love with him. She told him how she had decided to take matters into her own hands and go out to the Bible Institute to talk to Dr. Neilsen.

Slowly her husband drew the entire story from her. She told how she had led Dr. Neilsen to believe that Marilyn wasn't a fit applicant for the Bible school.

When she had finished, Harold Forester sat there, staring at her. Finally, he got to his feet.

"Get your coat, Carrie," he said harshly.

She stood beside him, trembling.

"What are we going to do?" she asked. "Where are we going?"

"We're going out to see Dr. Neilsen," he told her. "We're going out and you are going to tell him exactly the same things that you have just told me."

"But Harold – ," she protested.

He got her coat from the closet and held it for her. She wiped away the tears and slipped into it.

* * * *

The following morning Marilyn was getting ready for school when the telephone rang. She answered it reluctantly but began to smile as she talked. A moment later she hung up, her face radiant.

"Guess what?" she cried. "That was Dr. Neilsen! He said that they had almost made a terrible mistake. They are accepting me at the Bible school!"

"That's fine, darling," Harold Forester smiled. "I knew there must have been some mistake when I first learned that your application had been turned down."

"Now I can go to school with the rest of my friends," Marilyn said excitedly. "I'll be able to get the Bible background that I've been wanting and praying about." She turned to her mom, "Isn't it wonderful?"

"I am glad you were accepted, Marilyn," she managed.

When Marilyn was gone, running excitedly down the walk to the place where she and Kay used to meet to walk to school together, Mrs. Forester turned to Harold.

"I – I appreciate your not telling Marilyn what happened."

He smiled and took her by the shoulder. "I know you thought you were doing what was best for Marilyn," he said. "And you don't need to worry about her ever finding out about it from either Dr. Neilsen or myself."

"I can hardly stand to think of her throwing her life away like that," Mrs. Forester continued. "I wanted something better for her than that."

"My dear," Harold Forester answered softly, "there isn't anything better in all the world than what Marilyn's got in her heart right now. I used to feel the same way you do, before I confessed my sin and trusted Christ as my Savior. I used to think that going to church was a waste of time unless it helped business and that being a Christian was to be some sort of fanatic. It wasn't until I knew the Lord Jesus myself that I really found out how wrong I was."

THE DANNY ORLIS SERIES

The Danny Orlis series, by Bernard Palmer, delivers a blend of adventure, mystery, and suspense through various settings—from the Canadian wilderness to Guatemalan jungles. Danny Orlis, an adept outdoorsman, skilled athlete, and committed Christian, employs his quick thinking, calm bravery, and biblical solutions to confront everyday problems and hair-raising dangers. Early stories focus on Danny navigating school life, sports, and outdoor challenges, while in later books, Danny and his wife Kay provide wisdom and guidance to youngsters facing lifelike situations and challenges. Having sold over two million copies, this series has made Palmer a renowned author in Christian youth literature. Palmer is also the author of the Felicia Cartright series and various other series for Christian youth.

AVAILABLE FROM WWW.ANEKOPRESS.COM